OLD SONGS AND SINGING GAMES

COLLECTED AND EDITED

By

Richard Chase

DOVER PUBLICATIONS, INC.
NEW YORK

International Standard Book Number: 0-486-22879-7
Library of Congress Catalog Card Number: 72-85499

Manufactured in the United States of America
Dover Publications, Inc.
180 Varick Street
New York, N. Y. 10014

Foreword

THE songs in this book are the cultural property of all the people in America whose heritage is British. These songs are not "mountain music," although many of the people who have given us tunes or verses do live in the Appalachians. But there is a vast difference between the fine songs they have remembered and the "hill-billy" songs that have so recently assailed our ears. Social class distinctions do not exist in this music. It is found among all our people. It is becoming more and more apparent that this tradition exists nearly everywhere in America —in the lowlands as well as in the uplands, in cities as well as in the country, in Maine as well as in Virginia, in the Middle West, and in the Far West.

Throughout the world today there is a renewal of interest in racial cultures. Denmark, Finland, and Ireland have each recently had a Folk Renascence—a flowering of arts based on the deep-rooted cultures of their people. Here is shown indisputably the value of a return to sources that are germane and individual to the heritage of a people. As Vaughan Williams says, "An art must be a reflection of the whole life of a community." Only when his art is based on the cultural heritage of his race can an artist communicate genuine and unmistakable truths.

These songs and games vary slightly with every individual, family, or community that knows them, as a natural result of oral transmission. They grow and change with use. This book, therefore, is not offered as a final authority on any of the materials contained herein. It has been difficult, in fact, to choose from the wealth of living tradition at hand the most attractive versions. I have obviously not been able to study every extant variation: I have taken from every source available what seemed to me the best materials for this present use. Finality is not possible in these things, nor is it desirable. Better tunes, verses, or figures for certain of these songs or games quite possibly might appear in later series.

Acknowledgements as to source of materials and for permission to use certain tunes or texts appear with each song or game. I am especially indebted to John Powell, George Pullen Jackson, Annabel Morris Buchanan, Winston Wilkinson, and Hilton Rufty for their assistance in selecting materials and for their suggestions in preparing the manuscript; and to Berkeley Williams, Jr. for valuable aid in preparing this Foreword.

R. C.

Beech Creek, North Carolina
June 30, 1937

Note to Teachers

THIS book is arranged in a graded manner, the easier songs and games being in the first part and the more difficult ones in the latter pages. Teachers who are not accustomed to shape-notes need not be concerned because of this unfamiliarity, since the position of any note is, as explained below, unchanged. Teachers who are familiar with the seven-shape notation will be greatly aided, we believe, in understanding the structure of certain of the tunes.

These materials should probably be taught entirely by rote. We would recommend that the song or game to be taught should be mastered thoroughly beforehand by the teacher, so that it can be taught from memory. The interpretation should be simple and straightforward, with strict attention to time values. We have found it good practice to teach the words first, in exact rhythm but without the tune, and then to play the tune without any harmony and ask the children to think of the words. This concentrates the child's attention on the words and a new tune thus comes to him more easily.

We have not included piano accompaniments because the full educational value of this traditional music depends on two principles: 1. The character of the simple melodic line of the tune; and 2. The full use of the child's voice in singing. We would suggest that, if a piano is used to teach the songs, no attempt be made to furnish harmonies for any tunes other than those in the major scale. Proper harmonies for the other modes are difficult even for highly trained musicians.

Wherever verses other than the first might present difficulties in being fitted to the tune, bar markings have been indicated to aid in finding the right accent and the right notes.

Except where otherwise indicated, the tunes are in the usual major scale, or Ionian Mode.

John Powell, in his introduction to *Twelve Folk Hymns*, says,

Most fascinating in this folk-music is the use of the ancient modes, for three hundred years virtually forgotten in art music. The modes are scales of the same general type as our familiar major scale. The most usual can be formed by using the white keys only: The Ionian Mode, from C to C, is identical in the successive steps with the major scale; from D to D is the Dorian Mode; the Phrygian is from E to E; the Lydian from F to F; from G to G, the Mixolydian; from A to A, the Aeolian. It is immediately evident that the half-tone steps which come between the third and fourth and the seventh and eighth degrees of the major scale vary in position in each of these modes. The resulting unexpectedness of the intervals and emphasis on unusual degrees of the scale give these modal tunes their unparalleled charm and surprising originality.

CONCERNING THE SHAPE-NOTES

The tunes in this book are printed in shape-notes for the following reasons:

First, because this notation is known to many of the people from whom these songs have come, and because many of them have suggested that the seven-character notes be used in this book in order that they might read the tunes more easily;

Second, because round-note readers will lose nothing by this use of shape-notes, since the position of every note is exactly the same as in the regular notation;

Third, because the shape-note tradition is in itself worth encouraging as a simple aid to the sight-reading of music, especially for the sake of our people who have no access to any other musical training and to whom the seven-character notation is a necessity.

The seven-character notation is the same in principle as the tonic SOL-FA notation, but it facilitates learning to read the regular notation since the notes are always in position on the staff.

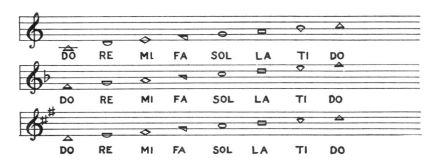

SPECIAL NOTE FOR READERS OF SHAPE-NOTES

Shape-note readers will understand Mr. Powell's explanation of the modes more clearly thus:

The Aeolian Mode has LA for its tonic, or key-note. Its "scale" is:

LA,   TI,   DO,   RE,   MI,   FA,   SOL,   LA

The Mixolydian Mode has SOL as its tonic:

SOL,   LA,   TI,   DO,   RE,   MI,   FA,   SOL

The Dorian Mode:

RE,   MI,   FA,   SOL,   LA,   TI,   DO,   RE

The Phrygian Mode:

MI,   FA,   SOL,   LA,   TI,   DO,   RE,   MI

You will already be familiar with LA as a key-note. The use of SOL, RE, and MI as key-notes is the best solution to the problem of *the modes in shape-notes,* because accidentals (*Ree, May, Say,* etc.) will be very rare, and the use of key-notes other than

ix

DO and LA seems natural and logical to the seven-character-note system in setting down modal tunes for singing "by shape."

Hitherto, no one has dealt with this particular problem with your needs in mind, although many of the "unwritten songs" of our people are *sung* in these modes. Even the rare Lydian Mode (tonic FA) has been found in use by singers of the old songs.

This special use of the seven-character notation has, in this book, no harmonic bearing but relates solely to melody. The problem of modal harmony is a difficult one and must await the attention of trained musicians of the future who will be in touch with your interests and will understand your love for the music that has been handed down to us and kept alive for untold generations—this "old music" that we and our children shall always enjoy and cherish.

Contents

xi

V. ROUND

VI. SINGING GAMES

VII. PLAY-PARTY GAMES

VIII. COUNTRY DANCE

OLD SONGS AND SINGING GAMES

The value of such songs as these as material for the general education of the young cannot be overestimated. For, if education is to be cultural and not merely utilitarian, . . . it will be necessary to pay at least as much attention to the training and development of the emotional, spiritual and imaginative faculties as to those of the intellect. And this, of course, can be achieved only by the early cultivation of some form of artistic expression, such as singing, which, . . . seems of all the arts to be the most natural and the most suitable one for the young. Moreover, remembering that the primary purpose of education is to place the children of the present generation in possession of the cultural achievements of the past so that they may enter as quickly as possible into their racial inheritance, what better form of music or of literature can we give them than the folk-songs and folk-ballads of the race to which they belong, or of the nation whose language they speak?

CECIL J. SHARP, in *English Folk Songs from the Southern Appalachians.*

Through this music, which has been a vital part of the daily life of our people through thousands of years, we are put into contact with our own lives in a mysterious and electrifying fashion. Human contacts become normal and natural, revivifying and inspiriting. The wisdom of simple ways is as apparent as it was to Cecil Sharp when he first made the acquaintance of the bearers of our musical heritage. We are a folk, and in that fact lies some of the secret of the Golden Age for which we seek through future and through past.

JOHN POWELL, in *Home and Garden Review.*

An art must be a reflection of the whole life of a community. Any direct and unforced expression of our common life may be the nucleus from which a great art will spring; of such expressions the folk song is the most genuine and the most unadulterated, besides being in itself a complete form of art.

R. VAUGHAN WILLIAMS, in *English Folk Songs.*

In the folk dances of their own race children have a form of artistic expression which must, from its very nature, be especially suited to them. Properly taught, dancing, though a recreation, inculcates the valuable lesson that discipline and restraint are needed in play no less than in work.

CECIL J. SHARP, in *Folk Dancing in Schools.*

The destiny of a nation depends on the dances of the people.

MOLIÈRE.

GO TELL AUNT RHODY

Verses selected and tune written down by Richard Chase

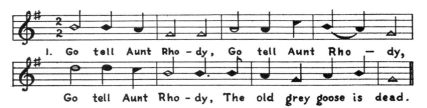

2. The | one that she's been | saving *(3 times)*
   To | make a feather | bed.

3. | She died in the | mill-pond
   | Standing on her | head.

4. The | goslings all are | cry-en
   To | think their mother's | dead.

5. The | gander is a- | mourn-en
   Be- | cause his wife is | dead.

6. The | barnyard is a- | weeping
   | Waiting to be | fed.

(Note: the "-en" of verses 4 and 5 are sung thus, and not "-ing.")
   This song is known in families all over America, rich and poor, town-folk and country-folk. Most of us were sung to sleep with the first two verses anyhow, or with

Bye lo, my baby,
Bye lo, my baby,
Bye lo, my baby,
Bye lo, baby, bye

to the same tune.

Many different "Aunts" appear in the tradition—Nancy, Rosie, Tabby, Abbie, Dinah, Patsy, etc. Sing your own favorite two-syllabled Aunt.

Verses 4 and 5 came from little Ruth Greer (8 years old) of Boone, North Carolina. She had learned them from her mother. Verse 6 is from a phonograph record. I cannot remember the source of verse 3. I first learned this song from Mrs. Neida Humphrey Pratt of Huntsville, Alabama.

This melody is also used as a hymn tune and as such is known as "Greenville" or "Rousseau's Dream." It was used in an opera written by Jean Jacques Rousseau in 1750. It is said that Rousseau dreamed that he was taken to heaven where he heard the angels singing this tune as they stood around the throne of God.

Whatever the origin of this simple melody, it has become dear to us in our own tradition by its use with these verses.

COCKY ROBIN

Verses selected by Richard Chase   *Tune written down by Cecil Sharp*

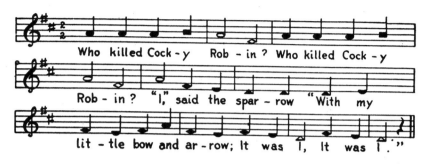

Who killed Cock-y Rob-in? Who killed Cock-y Rob-in? "I," said the spar-row "With my lit-tle bow and ar-row; It was I, It was I."

2. Who saw him die? *(2 times)*
    "I," said the fly,
    "With my little teency eye;
    It was I, it was I."

3. Who caught his blood?
    "I," said the fish,
    "With my little silver dish; . . ."

4. Who made his coffin?
    "I," said the snipe,
    "With my little pocket knife; . . ."

5. Who made his shroud-en?
    "I," said the beetle,
    "With my little sewing needle; . . ."

6. Who dug his grave?
    "I," said the crow,
    "With my little spade and hoe; . . ."

7. Who hauled him to it?
"I," said the bear,
"Just as hard as I could tear; . . ."

8. Who let him down?
"I," said the crane,
"With my little golden chain; . . ."

(Pat hands together, quietly.)

9. Who pat his grave?
"I," said the duck,
"With my | big old splattery | *foot;* . . ."
(The word "foot" is spoken with a single clap of hands.)

10. Who preached his funeral?
"I," said the swallow,
(Loud, but not too loud!)
"Just as *loud as I could holler!* . . ."

(10. *Alternative verse:*
Who preached his funeral?
"I," said the lark,
"With a song and a harp; . . .")

Mr. Sharp wrote down this tune from the singing of "Master William Agy at Barbourville, Kentucky, May 10, 1917."

The verses are from Ferry and Will Middleton, who live near Tuckasiegee, North Carolina, and from the Ward family of Beech Creek, North Carolina.

The tune is used by permission and by special arrangement with the Oxford University Press.

FROG WENT A-COURTING

Verses selected and tune written down by Richard Chase

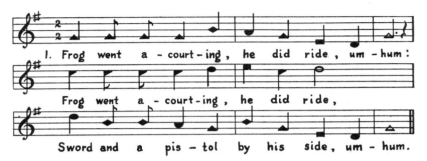

1. Frog went a-court-ing, he did ride, um-hum:
Frog went a-court-ing, he did ride,
Sword and a pis-tol by his side, um-hum.

2. | He rode down to Miss | Mousie's door . . . *(2 times)*
Where he'd often been before.

3. | Little Miss Mousie came | tripping down . . .
In her silk and satin gown.

4. | Then Miss Mousie | asked him in . . .
Where she sat to card and spin.

5. He | took Miss Mousie on his knee . . .
Said, "Miss Mousie, will you marry me?"

6. "With- | out my Uncle Rat's consent . . .
I | would not marry the Pres-i-dent."

7. | Soon Uncle | Rat came home . . .
"Who's been here since I been gone?"

8. | "Nice young man with a moustache on . . .
Asking me to marry him."

9. | Uncle Rat gave his consent, . . .
The | weasel wrote the publishment.

10. The | old Rat laughed till he | shook his fat sides . . .
To | think Miss Mousie would be a bride.

11. Oh | what will be the | wedding gown? . . .
A | piece of a hide of an old grey hound.

12. Oh where will the wedding supper be? . . .
| 'Way down yonder in a hollow tree.

13. Oh what will the wedding supper be? . . .
| Two butter beans and a black-eyed pea.

14. Oh the | first came in was a little white moth . . .
Spreading down the table cloth.

15. Oh the next came in was a bumble bee . . .
| Set his banjo on his knee.

16. Oh the next came in were two little ants . . .
Fixing around to have a dance.

17. Oh the next came in was the old grey goose . . .
Picked up her fiddle and she cut loose.

18. Oh the next came in was the muley cow . . .
Tried to dance but didn't know how.

19. Oh the next came in was a little old tick . . .
Walking around with his walking stick.

20. Oh the next came in was a little old gnat . . .
High-top shoes and a derby hat.

21. Oh the next came in was a betsy bug . . .
    Passing around the cider jug.

22. Oh the next came in was the old grey cat . . .
    Said she'd put an end to that.

23. | Bride went scrambling up the wall . . .
    | Her foot slipped and she got a fall.

24. | Frog went swimming a-| cross the lake . . .
    | He got swallowed by a big black snake.

25. | Song book sitting | on the shelf . . .
    If you | want any more you can | sing it yourself.

So many people, over such a long period of time, have contributed to this song as put together here, that I cannot remember all of them. The first I remember distinctly—Mrs. Charles Byers, of Chase, Alabama. More recent contributors are: Mrs. Zachary Moses (Glenville, North Carolina), Mr. Will Middleton (Tuckasiegee, North Carolina), children and citizens of Holly Grove, West Virginia, the Blair family (Banner Elk, North Carolina), and Miss Ida Lee Brady (Carthage, North Carolina). The tune given here is as sung by Mrs. Neida Humphrey Pratt, of Huntsville, Alabama.

There are many other verses, some of them very good ones, but twenty-five verses are quite enough. If you have any more, "you can sing them yourself!"

An excellent tune to "Froggy" is in John Powell's section of "Music Highways and Byways," in *The Bronze Book* (Silver, Burdett & Company, New York).

THE OAKUM IN THE WOODS

Verses written down by Richard Chase

*Tune written down by
Annabel Morris Buchanan*

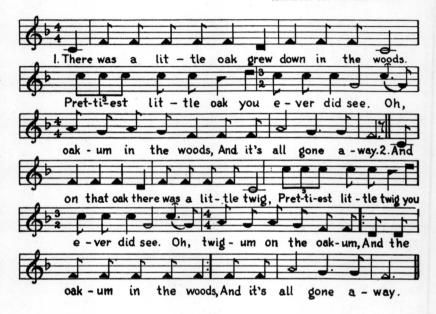

1. There was a lit — tle oak grew down in the woods.
Pret-ti-est lit — tle oak you e — ver did see. Oh,
oak — um in the woods, And it's all gone a -way. 2. And
on that oak there was a lit-tle twig, Pret-ti-est lit-tle twig you
e — ver did see. Oh, twig - um on the oak-um, And the
oak — um in the woods, And it's all gone a - way.

3. And on that twig there was a little leaf,
   Prettiest little leaf you ever did see.
   Oh, leaf on the twigum,
   And the twigum on the oakum,
   And the oakum in the woods,
   And it's all gone away.

4. And on that leaf there was a little nest . . .
   Oh, nestum on the leaf,
   And the leaf on the twigum. . . .

5. And in that nest there was a little egg . . .
Oh, eggum in the nestum,
And the nestum on the leaf. . . .

6. And in that egg there was a little bird . . .
Oh, birdum in the eggum,
And eggum in the nestum. . . .

7. And on that bird there was a little wing . . .
Oh, wingum on the birdum,
And birdum in the eggum. . . .

8. And on that wing there was a little feather . . .
Oh, feather on the wingum,
And wingum on the birdum. . . .

9. And on that feather there was a little spot,
Prettiest little spot you ever did see.
Oh, spotum on the feather,
And the feather on the wingum,
And the wingum on the birdum,
And the birdum in the eggum,
And the eggum in the nestum,
And the nestum on the *leaf,*
And the *leaf* on the twigum,
And the twigum on the oakum,
And the oakum in the woods,
And it's all gone away.

(Note: the "-um" tag is put on only in the cumulative part of the song, and it is omitted altogether for "feather" and "leaf.")

There are many versions of this song in both England and America. This tune came from Mrs. Phrony Trivitt, of Saint Clair's Creek, Virginia, and was written down August 21, 1936, by Annabel Morris Buchanan. The verses are from Mrs. Nancy Baldwin, whom I heard sing this song at the White Top Festival, August, 1934.

This tune is used by the kindness of Annabel Morris Buchanan, and may not be reproduced without her direct permission.

GROUND HOG

DORIAN MODE

Verses selected by Richard Chase   *Tune written down with the assistance of Hilton Rufty*

1. Whet up your knife and whis-tle up your dog, Whet up your knife and whis-tle up your dog; We're go-ing to the hol-ler to catch a ground hog. Ground hog!

2. Too many rocks and too many logs,   *(2 times)*
   Too many rocks to hunt ground hogs.

3. Over the hills and through the bresh . . .
   There we struck that hog-sign fresh.

4. Two in the clift and one in the log . . .
   I saw his nose and I knew he was a hog.

5. Up come Johnny with a ten-foot pole . . .
   To rouse that ground hog out of his hole.

6. Work, boys, work as hard as you can tear . . .
   The meat'll do to eat and the hide'll do to wear.

7. Took him by the tail and | pulled him out . . .
   Oh, my golly, ain't a ground hog stout!

8. Took him home and tanned his hide . . .
   Made the best shoestrings ever tied.

9. Put him in the pot and stuck it on to bile . . .
   You could smell that ground hog meat a mile.

10. Children all around they screamed and they cried . . .
    They love a ground hog stewed or fried.

11. Old Aunt Sally come a-skipping down the hall . . .
    We got enough whistle pig to feed them all.
    Whistle pig!

This tune came from Ollie Ward, of Beech Creek, North Carolina. The verses were selected from many sources, oral and printed. Boys all over the Appalachian Highlands know this song. It is usually sung in the major scale.

6

THE GOOD OLD MAN

FIVE-TONE AIR, APPARENTLY MIXOLYDIAN MODE

Verses selected by Richard Chase   *Tune written down by Cecil Sharp*

Where are you go - ing, my good old man? Where are you go - ing, my ho - ney, my lamb? Best old soul in the world.

(Spoken gruffly)   *Goin' huntin'!*

2. When will you be | back, my good old man? . . .
   Friday evenin'!

3. What'll you have for | supper? . . .
   Eggs!

4. How many will you | have? . . .
   Bushel!

5. A bushel will | kill you . . .
   Can't he'p it!

6. Where do you want to be | buried? . . .
   In the chimney corner!

7. Ashes will | fall on you . . .
   Don't care if they do!

8. Why do you want to be buried | there? . . .
   So I can ha'nt ye!

9. Ha'nt can't | ha'nt a ha'nt . . .
   Meanest old devil in the world!

Mr. Sharp collected a version of this song in England, but it was used there as a singing game. Another version of it has been found in Wales. It is rather widely known in America.

Verses 1 through 5 came from John Powell, and from Mrs. Betty Powell Brockenbrough (Mr. Powell's sister) of Richmond, Virginia. Verses 6 through 9 came from Mrs. Zachary Moses, of Glenville, North Carolina.

The tune came from Una and Sabrina Ritchie "at Hindman School, Knott County, Kentucky, September 20, 1917." It is used here by permission, and by special arrangement with the Oxford University Press.

THE MILLER'S THREE SONS

MIXOLYDIAN MODE

Verses selected by Richard Chase   *Tune written down with the assistance of Winston Wilkinson*

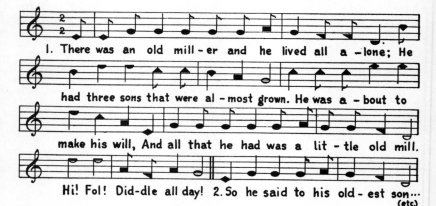

1. There was an old mill-er and he lived all a-lone; He had three sons that were al-most grown. He was a-bout to make his will, And all that he had was a lit-tle old mill. Hi! Fol! Did-dle all day! 2. So he said to his old-est son... *(etc)*

2. So he said to his oldest son,
    "Son, O son, I'm almost gone;
    And | if to you this mill I make,
    Pray | tell me the toll that you | mean to take."
    Hi! Fol! Diddle all day! *(Sung at the end of each verse.)*

3. "Father, you know my | name is Jack;
    | Out of a bushel | I'll take a peck;
    For | if my fortune | I would make,
    Oh, | that is the toll that I | mean to take.". . .

4. "Son, O son, I'm afraid you're a fool,
    You have not learned to follow my rule;
    To you this mill I will not give,
    For by such a toll no man can live.". . .

5. Then he said to his second son,
"Son, O son, I'm almost gone;
And if to you this mill I make,
Pray tell me the toll that you mean to take.". . .

6. "Father, you know my name is Ralph;
Out of a bushel I'll take a half;
For if my fortune I would make;
Oh, that is the toll that I mean to take.". . .

7. "Son, O son, I'm afraid you're a fool,
You have not perfect learned my rule;
To you this mill I will not give,
For by such a toll no man can live.". . .

8. Then he said to his youngest son,
"Son, O son, I'm almost gone;
And if to you this mill I make,
Pray tell me the toll that you mean to take.". . .

9. | "Father, you know my | name is Paul;
| Out of a bushel | I'll take it all,
| Take all the grain and | swear to the sack,
And | beat the farmer if | he comes back.". . .

10. | "Glory be!" the | old man says,
"I've | got one son that's | learned my ways!"
| "Hallelujah!" the | old woman cried,
And the | old man straightened out his | legs and he
died. . . .

Mr. E. E. Ericson, from whom this tune and all the verses but 4
and 7 came, is associate professor of English at the University of
North Carolina. He learned it in Nebraska when he was a boy.
There are two versions of it in Mr. Sharp's Appalachian collection
—one from Kentucky, the other from North Carolina. It has also
appeared in collections of English folk songs.

THE CAMBRIC SHIRT

Verses selected and tune written down by Richard Chase

1. As you go through yon-der town—Rose de Ma - ry and thyme!
Take this word to that young girl, If
she would be a true lov - er of mine.

2.   Tell her to make me a|cambric shirt
      Rose de Mary and thyme! *(Repeat, as second line of each verse.)*
   Without any seam or|needle work,
   Then she'll be a true lover of mine.

3.   Tell her to wash it in|yonder well . . .
   Where water never ran nor|rain never fell,
   Then she'll be a true lover of mine.

4.   Tell her to dry it|on a thorn . . .
   Where leaf never was since|Adam was born,
   Then she'll be a true lover of mine.

5.   I came back from|yonder town . . .
   She sent word to|that young man,
   If he would be a true lover of mine.

6.   Tell him to clear me an|acre of land . . .
   Between the sea and the|salt sea strand,
   Then he'll be a true lover of mine.

7. Tell him to plow it with a | muley cow's horn . . .
   And sow it all over with | one grain of corn,
   Then he'll be a true lover of mine.

8. Tell him to reap it | with a stirrup leather . . .
   And bind it all up with a | tomtit's feather,
   Then he'll be a true lover of mine.

9. Tell him to thresh it | in a shoe sole . . .
   And crib it all in a | little mouse hole,
   Then he'll be a true lover of mine.

10. Tell him when he's | done this work . . .
    Come to town and | get his shirt,
    Then he'll be a true lover of mine.

This tune and most of the verses came from Mrs. Fannie Norton, of Norton, North Carolina. Some of the verses came from the Mother Goose version, which has the refrain

Parsley, sage, rosemary and thyme!

Mrs. Norton's grandson, Hilton Norton (17 years old), who first told me about the song, had written down her refrain as follows:

Rose de Marian Time!

Since "thyme" is pronounced "time," it is my own guess that the refrain given with the song above may be nearer Mrs. Norton's original source.

This song is Number 2 in the Child Collection; it is one of the oldest in our language.

THE MARY GOLDEN TREE

DORIAN MODE

Verses selected by Richard Chase

Adapted from a tune collected by Cecil Sharp

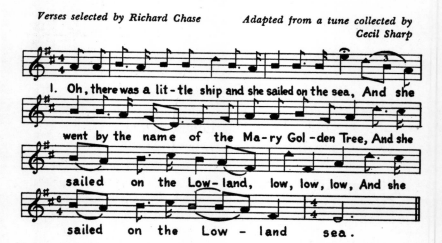

1. Oh, there was a lit-tle ship and she sailed on the sea, And she went by the name of the Ma-ry Gol-den Tree, And she sailed on the Low-land, low, low, low, And she sailed on the Low-land sea.

2. And there was another ship and she sailed upon the sea,
   And she went by the name of the Turkish Robbery,
   And she sailed on the Lowland, low, low, low,
   And she sailed on the Lowland sea.

3. And there was a little sailor un-|to the captain said,
   "O|captain, O captain, what|will you give to me,
   If I sink them in the Lowland, low, low, low,
   If I sink them in the Lowland sea?"

4. "Oh,|I will give you gold and|I will give you fee,
   And my|youngest pretty daughter for your|wedded
        wife to be,
   If you'll sink them in the Lowland, low, low, low,
   If you'll sink them in the Lowland sea."

5. The | boy leaped down and a- | way swam he,
   Till he | came to the ship of the Turkish Robbery,
   Where she sailed upon the Lowland, low, low, low,
   Where she sailed upon the Lowland sea.

6. Then | out of his pocket an | instrument he drew,
   And he | bored nine holes for to | let the water through,
   And he sunk them in the Lowland, low, low, low,
   And he sunk them in the Lowland sea.

7. He | turned upon his breast and | back swam he,
   Till | he came to the ship of the | Mary Golden Tree,
   Where she sailed upon the Lowland, low, low, low,
   Where she sailed on the Lowland sea.

8. "O | captain, O captain, won't | you take me on board?
   O | captain, O captain, won't | you be good as your
      word?
   For I've sunk them in the Lowland, low, low, low,
   For I've sunk them in the Lowland sea."

9. "O | no, I will neither take | you on board,
   O | no, I will neither be | good as my word,
   And I'm sailing on the Lowland, low, low, low,
   And I'm sailing on the Lowland sea."

10. "If it | wasn't for the love that I | have for your men,
    I would | do unto you as I've | done unto them,
    I would sink you in the Lowland, low, low, low,
    I would sink you in the Lowland sea."

11. He | turned upon his back and | down sank he—
    "Fa-re | well, fa-re well to the | Mary Golden Tree,
    For I'm sinking in the Lowland, low, low, low,
    For I'm sinking in the Lowland sea."

This tune came from Mr. William Wooten of Hindman, Kentucky. I heard this ballad first at Pine Mountain, Kentucky, but I cannot remember all the sources of the verses selected here. In the Child Collection, this song is Number 286.

The tune is used by permission, and by special arrangement with the Oxford University Press.

THE FARMER'S CURST WIFE

Verses selected by Richard Chase   *Tune written down by Winston Wilkinson*

1. There was an old farm-er lived un-der the hill—
(.......Whistled........) There was an old farm-er lived un-der the hill; He had a lit-tle farm and on it did dwell. Twice fa la, fa lil-ly, fa lay ri O!

2. The | devil came to him one | day at the plow . . .
Says, | "One of your family I'll | have to have now."
Twice fa la, fa lilly, fa lay ri O! *(Repeat at end of each verse.)*

3. "It's | neither your son nor your | daughter I crave . . .
But your | old scolding wife I | now must have.". . .

4. | "Take her, O take her with all my heart . . .
I hope you and she will never more part.". . .

5. So the | devil he bundled her | up in a sack . . .
And | slung her up a- | cross his back. . . .

6. He | carried her down to the | high gates of Hell . . .
Says, | "Poke up the fire boys, we'll | scorch her well.". . .

7. | Twelve little devils came | walking by . . .
She | up with her foot, kicked e- | leven in the fire. . . .

8. The | odd little devil peeped | over the wall . . .
Says, | "Take her back, daddy, she's a- | murderin' us all." . . .

9. The | poor old farmer he | looked through the crack . . .
And | saw the old devil a- | waggin' her back. . . .

10. The | poor old man he | lay sick in the bed . . .
She | upped with the butterstick and | paddled his head. . . .

11. And | now you see what a | woman can do . . .
She can | outdo the devil, and her | old man too. . . .

Mr. Wilkinson wrote down this tune from the singing of Miss Polly Morris of Pirkley, Greene County, Virginia. It is used here by his kindness and may not be reproduced without his direct permission.

Most of the verses came from Randolph Harrison (17 years old), of Cartersville, Virginia. He learned them from his father. Several verses came from Harton Barker, of Chilhowie, Virginia, and were furnished by Pat Campbell Buchanan, of Marion, Virginia, who had learned them from Mr. Barker. In the Child Collection, this song is Number 278.

THE TWELVE DAYS OF CHRISTMAS

AEOLIAN MODE

Verses selected by Richard Chase   *Tune found by Phillips Barry*

1. The first day of Christ-mas, My true love gave to me, A part-ridge in a pear tree.

2.   The second day of Christmas
   My true love gave to me

Two tur-tle doves, And a

partridge in a pear tree. *(As in verse 1)*

3.   The third day of Christmas
   My true love gave to me

Three French hens,

Two turtle doves, *(As in verse 2)*
And a partridge in a pear tree.

25

4. The fourth day of Christmas
   My true love gave to me

Four col – ly birds,

Three French hens, *(As in verse 3)*
Two turtle doves,
And a partridge in a pear tree.

5. The fifth day of Christmas
   My true love gave to me

Five gol – den rings ,

Four colly birds, *(As in verse 4)*
Three French hens,
Two turtle doves,
And a partridge in a pear tree.

6. The sixth day of Christmas
   My true love gave to me

six geese a lay – ing ,

Five golden rings, *(As in verse 5)*
Four colly birds,
Three French hens,
Two turtle doves,
And a partridge in a pear tree.

The melodic phrase for gifts 7 through 11 is now the same as for gift 6; the strains for gifts 5 back to 1 repeat each time as given above.

7. Seven swans a-swimming, . . .

8. Eight boys a-singing, . . .

9. Nine maids a-milking, . . .

10. Ten ladies dancing, . . .

11. E-|leven lords a-leaping, . . .

12. The twelfth day of Christ-mas, My true love gave to me,

Twelve bulls a – bel – low – ing, E –

leven lords a-leaping,
Ten ladies dancing,
Nine maids a-milking,
Eight boys a-singing,
Seven swans a-swimming,
Six geese a-laying,

Five gol-den rings, Four col- ly birds, Three French hens,

Two tur-tle doves, And a part-ridge in a pear tree

27

This tune was found by Dr. Barry in an old manuscript of 1790. It is used here by his kindness and may not be reproduced without his direct permission.

THE BLESSINGS OF MARY

MIXOLYDIAN MODE

Verses selected by Richard Chase   Tune written down by Gladys V. Jameson

1. The ve – ry first bless-ing that Ma – ry had, She had the bless-ing of one. To think that her son Je – sus Was God's e – ter – nal Son; Was God's e – ter – nal Son Like Em-man-u – el in glo – ry be Fa-ther, Son, and Ho – ly Ghost through all e – ter – ni · ty.

2.   The very next blessing that Mary had,
       She had the blessing of two:
       To think that her son Jesus
       Could read the Bible through:
       Could read the Bible through
       Like Emmanuel in glory be
       Father, Son, and Holy Ghost
       Through all eternity.

For each verse sing as verse 2, substituting the verse number for the last word in line two and the following lines for lines four and five in the verses indicated.

3. . . . Could make the blind to see. . . .

4. . . . Could turn the rich to poor. . . .

5. . . . Could raise the dead alive. . . .

6. . . . Could bear the crucifix. . . .

7. . . . Could open the gates of Heaven. . . .

Longer version:

7. . . . Could carry the keys of Heaven. . . .

8. . . . Could make the crooked straight. . . .

9. . . . Could turn the water to wine. . . .

10. . . . Could write without a pen. . . .

11. . . . Could open the gates of Heaven. . . .

12. . . . Could turn the sick to well. . . .

This tune was recorded from the singing of Darius Reece by Miss Jameson at Berea College. I first heard this carol, in oral tradition from Mary and Lucy Blair, of Banner Elk, North Carolina, who had learned it from Mr. Reece. Most of these verses are given as sung by these two little girls.

This carol goes back to the fifteenth century in England. See Number 70, "Joys Seven," in *The Oxford Book of Carols*.

This tune is used by the kindness of Gladys V. Jameson, and may not be reproduced without her direct permission.

13

THE HEBREW CHILDREN

APPARENTLY PHRYGIAN MODE WITH UNUSED SECOND—NO FA

Text from **The Sacred Harp**

Tune written down by
Annabel Morris Buchanan

Where now are the He-brew child-ren? Where now are the
He-brew child-ren? Where now are the He-brew child-rén?
Safe in the pro-mised land. Though the fur-nace
flamed a-round them, God while in their troub-les found them,
He with love and mer-cy bound them, Safe in the pro-mised land.

2. Where now are the twelve apostles? *(3 times)*
Safe in the promised land.
They went through the flaming fire,
Trusting in the great Messiah,
Holy grace did raise them higher,
Safe in the promised land.

3. Where now are the holy martyrs? *(3 times)*
Safe in the promised land.
Those who washed their robes and made them
White and spotless pure and laid them
Where no earthly stain could fade them,
Safe in the promised land.

4. Where now are the holy Christians? *(3 times)*
   Safe in the promised land.
   There our souls will join the chorus
   Saints and angels sing before us,
   While all heav'n is beaming o'er us,
   Safe in the promised land.

"The tune to this hymn as given in *The Sacred Harp* is slightly different from this version. The hymn is found in other old shape-note hymnals also. It is sometimes credited to Peter Cartwright, an early Southern camp-meeting preacher, who probably selected it from the 'unwritten music' of his people. The version here given was learned as a child from my grandfather, the Rev. J. R. Morris, of Huntsville, Alabama. The hymn is widely known among both white and Negro folk in the South, and has also been used as the basis of a college song, 'Where, O where are the verdant freshmen?' "

ANNABEL MORRIS BUCHANAN.

This tune is used by the kindness of Annabel Morris Buchanan and J. Fischer and Bro., and may not be reproduced without their direct permission.

14

O GENTLE SAVIOR

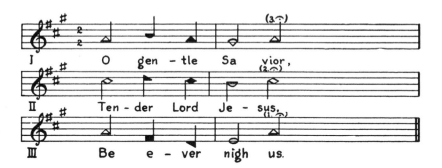

Sing once in unison. Then sing three times around; that is, group 1 begins, group 2 begins part I when group 1 gets to part II, and group 3 begins part I when group 2 gets to part II; but as group 1 ends the third time, group 2 ends on the second line, and group 3 ends on the first line, and all hold their ending note as marked above. In other words, group 1 sings the round three times entire, group 2 sings it two times and two-thirds, and group 3 sings it two times and one-third.

The original words for this round are:

> White sand and | grey sand. |
> Who'll buy my | white sand? |
> Who'll buy my | grey sand? |

I first heard this round in England, where it seems to be well known. I have not been able to trace its origin, except that in one little paper-backed book of songs for community singing, it was marked "Traditional English."

We used the words given here at the Morris Fork Community Center in Kentucky to open Sunday School and as a benediction after church, with the congregation singing the third part.

It is a good general practice in singing rounds to let the first group sing a round through as many times as there are parts (three times for a three-part round, four times for a four-part round), and to let the other groups end as the first group ends their last time. This means that in a four-part round, the fourth group will end on the first line; the third group, on the second line; the second group, on the third line; and the first group of course, on the fourth line.

15

THE FARMER'S IN THE DELL

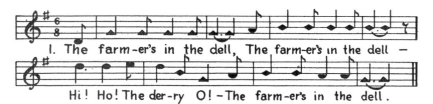

1. The farm-er's in the dell, The farm-er's in the dell —
Hi! Ho! The der-ry O! — The farm-er's in the dell.

2. The farmer takes a wife *(2 times)*
Hi! Ho! The derry O!
   (Repeat as third line of each verse)
The farmer takes a wife.
   *(First line of each verse serves also
   as last line)*

3. The wife takes a child. . . .

4. The child takes a nurse. . . .

5. The nurse takes a dog. . . .

6. The dog takes a bone. . . .

7. The bone stands alone. . . . *(walking)*

8. The bone stands alone. . . . *(skipping)*

9. We'll all clap the bone. . . .

For a large ring this longer version may be used:

6. The dog takes a cat. . . .

7. The cat takes a rat. . . .

8. The rat takes a cheese. . . .

9. The cheese takes a knife. . . .

10. The knife stands alone. . . . *(walking)*

11. The knife stands alone. . . . *(skipping)*

12. We'll all clap the knife. . . .

ACTION:

All join hands and form a ring around one child who stands in the center—"the farmer."

1. The ring moves to the left with a walking step.

2. The "farmer" chooses a "wife" from the moving ring, and stands with her right hand in his left.

3-6. Each child that is taken in takes another as the song directs, and one by one join hands to form a horseshoe on the farmer's left.

7. The "bone" (or in the longer version the "knife") is now encircled by the farmer, closing the horseshoe to make an inner circle around him, and this ring now moves to the right, still with a walking step.

8. Both rings now skip.

9. All the players close in around the bone (or knife) and clap in rhythm over his head.

All circle up again around the one left in the center, who becomes the farmer for the next round of the game.

It was in Cullowhee, North Carolina, that someone circled up inside the big ring and did this double circle ending. I had never seen it done before. It seems to add a fresh interest to this old game.

16

OATS AND BEANS

Verses and tune written down by Cecil Sharp

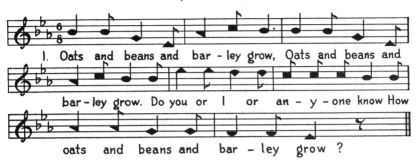

1. Oats and beans and bar-ley grow, Oats and beans and bar-ley grow. Do you or I or an-y-one know How oats and beans and bar-ley grow?

2. First the farmer sows his seed,
  Then he stands and takes his ease,
  Stamps his foot and claps his hand,
  And turns around to view the land.

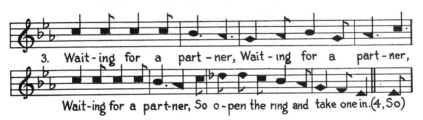

3. Wait-ing for a part-ner, Wait-ing for a part-ner, Wait-ing for a part-ner, So o-pen the ring and take one in. (4, So)

4. *(Same tune as verses 1 and 2)*
  So now you're married you must obey,
  You must be true to all you say,
  You must be wise, you must be good
  And help your wife to chop the wood.

ACTION:
 Circle up around one child and then let go hands.
 1. Circle to the left, single file, clapping hands and walking in time. All stop and face center at the end of the verse.

2. Line 1—vigorous sowing gesture.
    "   2—fold arms.
    "   3—stamp the right foot on the word "stamp"; clap hands
        on the word "clap."
    "   4—all turn once around clockwise with four little steps,
        shading the eyes with the right hand.

3. The ring now joins hands, but remains standing. The one in the center walks around the ring, counter-clockwise, and takes a partner on the last line of the verse.

4. The ring skips to the left. The two inside join crossed hands (R in R and L in L) and skip in the other direction, keeping as close to the ring as possible.

From *Children's Singing Games,* Set I, edited by Alice B. Gomme and Cecil J. Sharp (Novello's School Songs, Book 198). The action given here has been adapted from the playing of children in North Carolina. Used by permission of Novello and Company, Ltd., London.

17

DRAW A BUCKET OF WATER

Written down by Richard Chase

Draw a buck-et of wa-ter For the farm-er's daugh-ter.
One in a bush, and two in a bush, And the
first old la - dy pop un - der the bush.

This is sung four times thus; then a fifth time, a little faster, with the following serving as the last line:

And we'll all go 'round the mulberry bush.

ACTION:

For four players: Each couple joins hands straight across (R in L and L in R, facing each other), one couple having their hands above the other couple's hands.

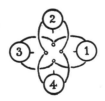

Players push their hands back and forth in time with the singing. They should be moved from the shoulders, elbows bent; that is, *not* moving the body. At the end of the first time, players 2 and 4 raise their joined hands and lower the arch behind player 1.

Second time: Player 3 "pops under" the same way.

Third time: Player 2 pops under.

Fourth time: Player 4 pops under.

Fifth time: All hop around to the left, on *both* feet. Bend slightly backward to keep "the basket" stretched into a proper circle.

It is possible to play this game with eight players standing thus:

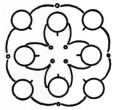

Move the hands up and down in this case, instead of back and forth. The players in the outside ring pop under in turn. The ending for the fifth time is the same.

This game is widely used. It is given here as I have seen it done in North Carolina.

18

THE NOBLE DUKE OF YORK

Verses selected and tune written down by Richard Chase

1. Oh, the no-ble Duke of York, He had ten thou-sand men; He led them up to the top of the hill, And he led them down a-gain.

2. Now | when they were up, they were | up,
   And | when they were down, they were | down,
   But | when they were only | halfway up
   They were | neither up nor | down.

3. Oh, a-hunting we will go,
   A-hunting we will go,
   We'll | catch a little fox and | put him in a box,
   And | then we'll let him | go.

ACTION:

For 5 or 6 couples in a line, with a space of 6 feet left open between the boys' file and the girls' file.

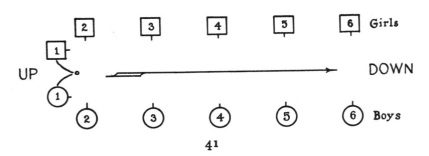

Verse 1: First couple *walks* 8 counts down the middle and 8 counts back, with inside hands joined each time. They turn back on the word "men."

Verse 2: First couple (partners facing each other) joins hands straight across (girl's right hand in boy's left and her left in his right) and *skips,* turning clockwise, down the middle to the bottom place, where they make an arch. In doing this be sure to use the whole 16 counts of the verse. And you must be careful not to turn counter-clockwise! This is "widdershins," and if you ever do anything widdershins you are almost sure to have some bad luck!

Verse 3: All the other couples take crossed hands (R in R and L in L) and facing the top, follow the top couple who turn short to their left ("First couple *cast off* to the left, all follow"), *skip* down below the arch, returning up the middle under it to places again with, now, a new top couple.

Repeat until each couple has been at the top.

When the last couple has done its figure and made its arch at the bottom, the original first couple makes an arch next to this last one immediately after passing under it; and each of the other couples makes an arch the same way *after* passing under *all* the other arches. Sing verse 3 for these ending arches.

The tune is given here as sung by Harlan Riley (11 years old), of Morris Fork, Kentucky. The action has been adapted from Gomme and Sharp (*Children's Singing Games,* Set II), and from various American play-party games.

19

O BELINDA

Verses selected and tune written down by Richard Chase

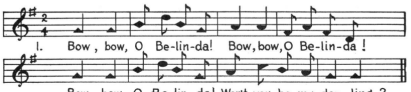

1. Bow, bow, O Be-lin-da! Bow, bow, O Be-lin-da!
Bow, bow, O Be-lin-da! Won't you be my dar-ling?

2. Right hand 'round, O Belinda. *(3 times)*
Won't you be my darling? *(Repeat at end of each verse.)*

3. Left hand 'round, O Belinda. . . .

4. Both hands 'round, O Belinda. . . .

5. Shake that big foot, shy all around her. . . .

6. Roll under, O Belinda. . . .

ACTION:

For 5 or 6 couples longways (the same as for "The Noble Duke of York").

Verse 1: First boy and last girl move (4 counts) toward each other and move (4 counts) *backwards* to places; then first girl and last boy do the same. Use a quiet, but jaunty and quick, walking step for verses 1 through 5.

Verse 2: First boy and last girl move forward and turn each other (clockwise) with right hands (8 counts); first girl and last boy do the same.

Verse 3: As before, with left hands, turning counter-clockwise.

Verse 4: As before, with both hands straight across, turning clockwise.

Verse 5: "Back to back": move forward, pass right shoulder to right shoulder, move around each other, and then move backward to places. Be careful to face the same way throughout—that is, do not turn around, but move backward to place.

Verse 6: All take hands and, following top couple, cast off (*skipping step*—see "The Noble Duke of York") to the left, returning up the middle to places, whereupon all raise their hands in arches. First couple then moves down under the arches to the bottom place. Try to perform all of this by the end of the verse. The first couple usually goes under while some of the couples are still moving.

Repeat until each couple has been at the top.

I learned this game first in New York City. It is played in Tennessee as "O Betty Liner." The version given here is from near Marion, North Carolina.

20

WEEVILY WHEAT

AEOLIAN MODE

Verses selected by John Powell *Tune written down by Winston Wilkinson*

(Verse No 2.) 1.Char-lie's neat and Char-lie's sweet, Char-lie is a dan-dy;

Char-lie is a nice young man, He feeds the girls on can-dy.

(Refrain) Rise you up in the morn-ing, All to-ge-ther ear-ly; You

need not feel at all a-fraid, In-deed I love you dear-ly.

2. Your|weevily wheat's not fit to eat,
Neither is your barley;
What I want is the best of rye
To bake a cake for Charlie.

(Refrain)

3. |Charlie is a brave young man,
Charlie is a soldier,
Sword and pistol by his side,
His musket on his shoulder.

(Refrain)

ACTION:

Longways for 5 or 6 couples (the same as for "O Belinda").

Verse 1: First couple takes both hands, straight across, and "sashay" (that is, move sideways with slipping steps) down the middle (8 counts) and back again (8 counts).

Verse 1, Refrain: Begin the Reel—first couple turns clockwise once and a half, hooking right elbows. Then first boy turns the second girl, hooking left elbows, counter-clockwise once around; while first girl turns the second boy the same way. Then first couple turn each other once around again with right elbows; then turn the third couple in line with left elbows, etc., etc., continuing to the last couple. Be sure that the "reeling" couple always does a complete *right* elbow swing with each other and that each of them does a complete *left* elbow swing with the next in line. And be sure that no unnecessary turning around is done in the Reel—that is, go *straight* from one turn to the next. Use a quiet, jaunty, *walking step* throughout the Reel.

When the reeling couple reaches the bottom place, they stay there and make an arch, the boy standing on his proper side.

Use verses 2 and 3 for the Reel, and try to finish the reeling just before the refrain of verse 3, then

Verse 3, Refrain: The boys' line casts off to the left, the girls' line casts off to the right; partners meet below the arch and come back up the middle to places. Use an easy *skipping step* throughout this verse.

Repeat until each couple has done all the figures. With the last time, the "finishing arches" may be done as in "The Noble Duke of York."

Mr. Powell selected these verses from the singing of Mr. J. H. ("Uncle Jim") Chisholm and Mrs. Victoria Morris, of Albemarle County, Virginia. Mr. Wilkinson wrote down the tune from Mr. Chisholm's singing. In the third lines of verses 2 and 3, I have made slight changes from Mr. Powell's version.

This tune and these verses are used by the kindness of Winston Wilkinson and John Powell, and may not be reproduced without their direct permission.

21

THE BEAR WENT OVER THE MOUNTAIN

Verses selected and tune written down by Richard Chase

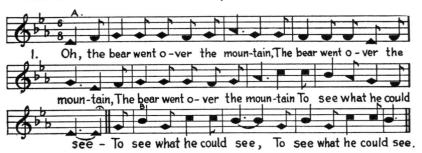

Second and third verses follow the exact pattern of the first. On the last round of figures, omit the B part of the third verse.

2. A. The other side of the mountain *(3 times)*
   Was all that he could see.
   B. Was *all* that *he* could *see.* *(2 times)*

3. A. Oh, we won't go home until morning *(3 times)*
   And maybe not at all.
   B. And *may*be *not* at *all.* *(2 times)*

ACTION:

Longways for any number of couples. To find numbers at the start, all take right hands across, beginning with top two couples; couples on the top side of each two-couple set are first couples, the others are second couples.

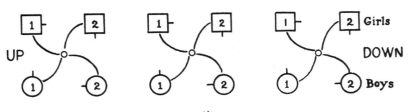

47

Verse 1. A. Right hands across (8 counts) and left hands back (8 counts), by all first and second couples. That is, first boy takes second girl by right hand, while second boy does same with first girl (as shown by crossed lines in diagram). Then this wheel moves 8 counts clockwise, all change to left hands and wheel moves back counter-clockwise 8 counts to places. The step used in this figure should be an easy *spring.* Do not lift the knees. Keep the feet under the body and bounce quietly forward from step to step.

B. All face partners in line and clap hands three times and three times again on words italicized above.

Verse 2. A. All first couples join right hands and *walk* 8 counts down the middle between second couples who stand still. On counts 7 and 8, first boys turn their partners under their right arm (girls turn *out,* to the left); then first couples join crossed hands and immediately, on the next count of 1, *skip* 8 counts back up the middle, continuing around their own second couples and ending in the second couples' place; *all* second couples moving up to first couples' place on last four counts.

B. All clap as before.

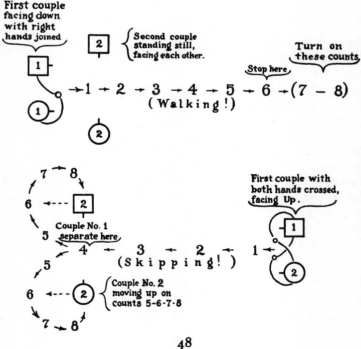

Verse 3. A. All turn partners, both hands straight across. Arms should not be bent nor kept rigid, but partners should lean back from each other enough to get a good balance for swinging. Use a quiet *skipping step.*

B. Each first couple takes right hands across with the *next* second couple *below.* All shake hands then on the same counts as for the clapping; and then—

Repeat from the beginning as many times as desired.

Progression and the changing of numbers

First couples aways move *down,* and second couples move *up* at the end of the A part of the second verse. Second couples, on reaching the top, stay out ("neutral") for one full round of the three verses, then they shake hands (on the B part of verse 3) with the next second couple *that moves up.* This means that the neutral couple at the *top* will change to a *first* couple when they are taken in. This progression and change of number works the same way at the bottom—that is, first couples go out at the bottom, stay neutral one full round, and then are taken in again as second couples.

This is only one of a good number of English country dances that are in this same "longways for as many as will" formation, and involve this same general kind of figure-pattern.

This country dance is used by permission of Novello and Company, Ltd., London.